DANNY'S DOODLES

LAP

DISCARD

The Jelly Bean Experiment

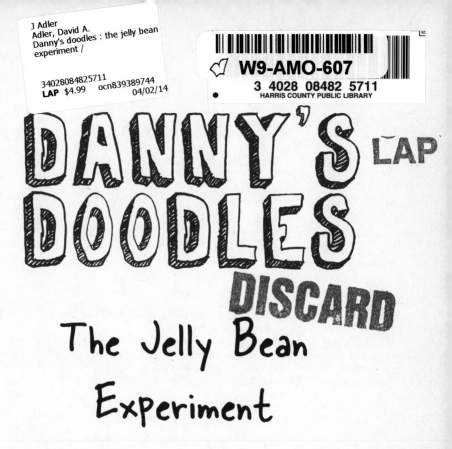

Story and illustrations by
David A. Adler

sourcebooks
jabberwocky

For my great nieces and nephews
Netanel, Emuna, Avital, Techiya,
Elyada, and Aviya.

Published by Sourcebooks Jabberwocky, an imprint of Sourcebooks, Inc.
P.O. Box 4410, Naperville, Illinois 60567-4410
(630) 961-3900
Fax: (630) 961-2168
www.jabberwockykids.com

Library of Congress Cataloging-in-Publication data is on file with the publisher.

Source of Production: Versa Press, East Peoria, Illinois, USA
Date of Production: June 2013
Run Number: 20688

Printed and bound in the United States of America.
VP 10 9 8 7 6 5 4 3 2 1

Contents

~~~~~~

I doodle when I write.
So here's the story
with all my doodles.

-Danny

Chapter 1

MONDAY AND THE JELLY BEANS

I am the subject of Calvin Waffle's experiment.

Last week at school he followed me everywhere. He didn't stay close, but he was there. Lurking. He made a list of everyone who walked up to me, everyone who spoke to me. He listed their names and how long we talked.

"What's with all the names and numbers?" I asked.

"I need them for my experiment," Calvin told me. "They're statistics, the backbone of science."

No, they're not, I thought. *The backbones of*

science are test tubes and microscopes and jars of chemicals, stinky chemicals that make your hands turn colors.

I know what statistics are. They're the backbone of sports. I know baseball batting averages, football passing and rushing records, and basketball shooting percentages.

Here's a statistic: My new friend Calvin Waffle is 100% weird.

All last week he followed me and lurked. Now it's Monday. We're on our way to school and he has that list. It's in his shirt pocket. It's folded and sticking up a bit like a fancy handkerchief.

"Are you going to keep watching who talks to me?"

Calvin shakes his head way up and down. He's nodding, telling me he'll keep watching.

2

"Last week was the control," he
says. "This week is the experiment."

I haven't known Calvin very
long. The first time we talked was
two weeks ago. It was after school.
I was walking home when he
called to me.

Two kinds of breakfast
waffles: A breakfast waffle
with syrup

"Hey. You're in my class."

I turned and saw him walking toward me.

"I'm Calvin Waffle," he said.

I knew that. I was there when our teacher
Mrs. Cakel introduced him to our class.

I told him my name. "I'm Danny Cohen."

Now we walk together to school and
back. That's because he lives on my block.

A Calvin
Waffle

He moved here with his mom. I don't know
about his father. I didn't ask. I never ask those
kinds of questions. I'm not a nosy news reporter.
I'm just a kid in the fourth grade. When I'm
older, I'll be a cartoonist.

It's Monday. We're about to turn the corner to

enter the school playground and Calvin stops. He pulls on my sleeve and says, "Come with me."

I follow him behind a big tree. Calvin takes a few large bags of jelly beans from his book bag. He fills my shirt pocket and my front and back pants pockets with beans.

"Thanks for the treats," I say.

"You can't eat any," Calvin tells me. "That would ruin it."

"Eating a few jelly beans would ruin what?"

"The experiment."

"What experiment?"

"I can't tell you that," Calvin says and shakes his head. "If I told you, I would ruin the experiment."

"What *can* you tell me?"

"Life is a mystery."

So are you, Calvin Waffle.

I look down at my bulging shirt pocket. Two red beans and a yellow look up at me.

"I might not be able to control myself," I say.

"Reds are my favorites. During class I might be tempted to dip into my pocket and take a snack."

Here is my pocket filled with beans.

"I'll know if any are missing," he says. He shows me the empty jelly bean bags and the number of the weight of the beans in the bag. "If they weigh less at the end of the day, I'll know you ate some."

"Or maybe," I say, "some fell out of my pockets."

I jump and a few beans fall out.

"Don't do that," Calvin says and picks up the jelly beans that fell. "You'll skew the experiment."

"Skew?"

"Change."

The bell rings. It's time to line up and go into school. Calvin puts the beans that fell back in my pocket. I hurry through the playground. Then I turn to tell Calvin

5

not to worry, that I'll try not to skew anything, but he isn't there. I'm near the front of the line and he's all the way in the back. Lurking.

I walk into class and my teacher Mrs. Cakel says, "Daniel, you're leaking."

I look down. Jelly beans. I turn. Behind me is a trail of beans. I bend to get them and more fall from my pockets. One by one I pick them up and drop them in my book bag.

I'm near the door, grabbing a green bean when Calvin walks into the room. He gives me a handful of beans I had dropped. I put them in my book bag and go to my seat.

I look up at nice Mrs. Cakel.

That's a joke.

Mrs. Cakel is not nice at all.

Her name is pronounced like cake with an added L at the end, but she's no sweet dessert. She's tough. On the side of the room, near

6

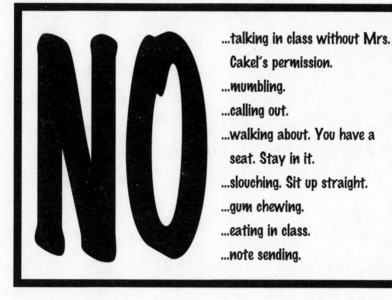

...talking in class without Mrs. Cakel's permission.

...mumbling.

...calling out.

...walking about. You have a seat. Stay in it.

...slouching. Sit up straight.

...gum chewing.

...eating in class.

...note sending.

where I sit, is a big NO sign. The NO is about a foot high and next to it are line after line of things you're not allowed to do in her class.

That NO sign is a challenge to Calvin. I bet every morning he thinks of how many of the NOs he can do without getting caught. Calvin and Mrs. Cakel are not a good match. They're like an onion and ice cream. In case you're wondering, Cakel is the onion.

Their problems started on Calvin's very first

day in class. He was standing near her desk and waiting to be seated. He looked at the NO sign and said, "It's lucky she allows breathing."

"What?" Mrs. Cakel asked. "Did you say something?"

Calvin put his feet together like he was a soldier. He looked straight ahead and said, "No, ma'am. I didn't say anything."

"Yes, you did but you mumbled." Mrs. Cakel pointed to the sign. "That's rule number two. No mumbling. And there's no talking here without my permission. That's rule number one. Do you understand?"

Calvin shook his head way up and down. He was nodding, telling her he understood the "No Talking" rule.

Calvin stood there with his feet together. "Are you chewing gum?"

His head went way up and way down. He was nodding.

MUMBLE!
MUMBLE!
MUMBLE!
MUMBLE!
MUMBLE!
MUMBLE!
MUMBLE!
STOP!
A MUMBLE BEE

"That's rule number six. No gum chewing."

Mrs. Cakel held the garbage pail under his chin and he dropped the gum in.

"Study that," she said and pointed to the NO sign.

She showed him to his desk. He sits in the back of the room. I sit near the front.

What else has Calvin done?

He made an origami bird from a homework assignment. He used a red crayon to answer the questions on a history test. He took off his sneakers and counted his toes during a math lesson.

I bet if Aladdin appeared in Cakel's class and said, "You have three wishes," her first wish would be, "Get that Waffle out of my class!"

Calvin usually sits with me during lunch, but not today. He's a few tables away. That's because of the jelly beans. He's watching me and taking notes.

Later, on the way home from school, I ask him about the experiment.

"I'm still gathering data," he answers.

"Data?"

"Numbers. Statistics."

"I know about statistics," I say. "They're the backbone of science."

"Yes, they are," Calvin says.

We stop by the front walk of his house and he has me empty my pockets. He puts the jelly beans back in their bags.

"I'll need them tomorrow," Calvin says.

He closes the tops of the bags with plastic ties.

Calvin's House.

"Only four more days," Calvin tells me, "and the experiment will be done. Then I'll tell you the results."

I say goodbye to Calvin and go home. I get in and go straight to the kitchen. I put my school things on the table and prepare a snack. Juice and jelly beans, the ones in my book bag. Calvin forgot about them.

Chapter 2

TUESDAY AND ANNIE ABRAMS

On the way to school I tell Calvin about our baseball team.

"You should join or at least come to our next game. We're playing the Robins. Whoever wins will be in first place."

"Robins! Why do they give teams bird names? What's your team? I bet it's another bird."

"I play third base."

"Come on. What is it? Blue Jays? Cardinals? Woodpeckers?"

"Eagles."

Calvin shakes his head and tells me, "I can't think

about baseball. I've got bigger problems. Mom told me I should have some friends over. She already baked a cake."

"You can serve jelly beans," I say.

"Food is not the problem. Friends are. You're my only one and I only know you because we're neighbors."

"Join the Eagles and you'll make friends."

"I'm not into bats and balls and wearing a flannel shirt with a number on the back. I need some friends to eat Mom's cake."

"It's your fault," I tell him. "I wanted to introduce you to some kids but you said, 'I'm not ready. I'm still observing the natives.' Now you have this crazy jelly bean thing and at lunch you don't even sit with me and my friends."

Calvin says, "That would skew the statistics."

"And statistics are the backbone of science," I say.

12

"Exactly."

We're close to school. He loads my pockets with jelly beans. The bell rings and I get in line. I don't turn and look for Calvin. I know he's way in the back watching me.

It feels weird being the subject of an experiment.

I bet that's how George Washington Carver's peanuts felt.

Carver did experiments with peanuts. He found lots of ways to use them like making them into gunpowder.

Well, right now I'm Calvin Waffle's peanut.

All through class I think about jelly beans and peanuts. It makes me hungry.

Just before lunch Mrs. Cakel tells us about a school project.

"You'll work in teams of

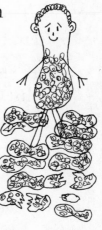

Me as a peanut with some of my friends.

13

two. Each team will report on a great figure in history. Each member of the team will report on a different time in the person's life."

She opens her marking book.

"We'll go in alphabetical order. Annie Abrams, you're first. Who do you want to be your teammate?"

My last name is Cohen. I'm next. I decide to choose Calvin. Annie looks at me and smiles.

"I pick Daniel," she says.

That's okay. She's a good student. Our team will do well. But what will happen to Calvin? Who will choose him? Mrs. Cakel gives Annie a sealed envelope.

"Don't open it," she tells Annie.

One by one Mrs. Cakel goes through the alphabet until she gets to Douglas Miller, the last one to choose a partner. There is only one kid left.

14

Douglas turns, points, and says, "I'll take him, Alvin."

No, I think. *His name is Calvin.* But I don't say that out loud. You don't say things out loud in Mrs. Cakel's class.

Mrs. Cakel says, "The teams will meet after lunch, but right now you may open your envelopes."

I watch as Annie tears open our envelope. She takes out a piece of paper, reads it, and then holds it up for me to see.

GEORGE WASHINGTON, SOLDIER AND PRESIDENT

Janet who sits next to me gets Louis Braille. Perry who sits in front of me gets Helen Keller. Jacob gets Harriet Tubman. Douglas gets Benjamin Franklin. That means Calvin also got Franklin.

Douglas's paper says:

BENJAMIN FRANKLIN, SCIENTIST AND STATESMAN

The bell rings. It's time for lunch.

15

"That Douglas doesn't even know my name," Calvin whispers to me on the way to the cafeteria. "He thinks I'm Alvin!"

"Benjamin Franklin is great for you," I say. "He did experiments."

"With jelly beans?" Calvin asks.

"No, with keys and kites and lightning."

And then Calvin is gone.

It's the beans. He can't sit with me during lunch and ruin the statistics.

I sit at my regular table, the one nearest the window. Annie sits next to me. She opens her lunch bag. "I have a cupcake. Do you want half?"

"No, thank you."

Annie takes out the cupcake, an apple, a container of juice, and a salami sandwich. She bites into the sandwich. Then she turns to me and asks, "Don't you want to say something to me?

"Thank you for picking me?"

"No. Something else."

Rinse out your mouth. You smell like salami. That's what I think, but I don't say it.

She points her sandwich at my shirt pocket.

"I said you could have half of my cupcake. Don't you want to give me some of your jelly beans?"

I can't answer. My mouth is full of pretzels. I just shake my head. No.

Annie's apples — The sguiggly things are the worms.

Annie says, "I like the green ones."

I swallow and tell her about Calvin's experiment.

"That's all too weird," Annie says. "What could he learn from jelly beans?"

I look at Calvin. He's writing in that little pad of his.

I tell Annie about Carver's peanuts and Franklin's kite.

"People can make great discoveries from

17

simple things. Maybe one day some fourth grader will be writing a report on Calvin Waffle."

That's what I said, but I don't believe it. I agree with Annie. This is all too weird.

In the afternoon Mrs. Cakel tells us about our reports.

"Next Monday each team will present two reports on each subject. I expect you to work together. Each of you will present one side of your subject."

She means one of us will report on Washington as soldier. The other will report on him as president.

Then Mrs. Cakel tells us, "Each team will get one grade."

"No!" Douglas calls out.

Mrs. Cakel glares at him.

"Sorry," Douglas whispers.

On the way home from school I think Calvin and I will talk about the reports. We don't.

18

"My family name wasn't always Waffle," Calvin says.

I had wondered about that.

"It started with a W and had lots of Ys and Zs in it. When Dad came here from Europe, he found that no one here could pronounce his name."

We stop in front of his house.

"He decided to change it to a real American name, one that started with W."

I say, "He could have changed it to Ward, Weber, or Wagner."

Calvin shakes his head.

"He wanted something people would like. He saw boxes of frozen waffles in a supermarket. 'What are those?' he asked a woman. 'They're waffles,' she said. 'Everyone loves waffles.'

"'That was it,' Dad told me. 'From then on our name was Waffle.'"

Then Calvin tells me why I never met his father.

"He speaks lots of languages. That's how he got his job."

Calvin takes the empty jelly bean bags from his book bag. I empty my pockets. It feels good not to be carrying around all those beans.

"He travels a lot for his work."

Calvin looks all around. He leans real close and whispers, "He's a spy."

Calvin walks toward his front door.

I just stand there.

A spy!

Calvin turns and waves to me. Then he goes into his house.

A spy, I think as I walk home.

In school Calvin lurks like a spy. Maybe he learned that from his dad.

A spy, I think again. *That's so exciting!* I live on the same block as a spy named Waffle.

20

Chapter 3

~~~~~~~~~~~~~~~~~~~~~~~~~~~~~~~

TUESDAY AFTERNOON, WEDNESDAY, AND THE BIG GREEN SPLOTCH

Do you know what happens to jelly beans when they go through the wash? They get wet and sticky. Do you know what happens to them when they're ironed? They get wet, sticky, big, and flat. And Mom says they ruin clothes.

"Look at this," she says when I walk in the house.

She holds up a pair of pants. My pants.

I look.

There's a large green splotch by one of the front pockets.

My splotched pants.

Mom shows me the back of the pants.

There's a yellow and orange splotch by one of the back pockets.

She unwraps some aluminum foil and shows me three squashed and ironed jelly beans. Green, yellow, and orange.

"These pants are ruined," Mom says. "Now, please explain to me why there were jelly beans in your pockets."

"I can still wear those pants."

"You're not wearing dirty pants to school."

She just stands there staring at me.

"What?" I ask.

Mom points to the large green splotch.

"Tell me about the beans?"

I put my books down. I tell her about Calvin Waffle and his jelly bean experiment.

"That's behavioral science," Mom says. "That's not my field."

Mom is a chemical engineer. I don't

22

know exactly what she does, just that she
works three days a week in a laboratory. I was
there a few times and wasn't allowed
to touch anything.

It's like when I visit Dad's Aunt
Ella. Before we go in Dad reminds
me not to touch things. He tells me,
"She has lots of valuable antiques."

Antiques are old stuff. Aunt Ella's
antiques are glasses and dishes and
vases. I guess she got them when
she was young and then just kept
them. She got old and her things
got old. Dad said, "That's what
happens."

AUNT ELLA

"It's not Calvin's fault your pants are
ruined," Mom tells me. "You were the one
who didn't empty your pockets before you put
your pants in the hamper."

It might be my fault, I think, *but those are
Calvin's beans.*

23

The next morning I tell Calvin about the splotches.

"That's great," Calvin says. "Your mom should iron lots more beans on those pants. It would be your splotch pair. Colorful and sticky. You could wear them to parties and sleepovers."

Calvin might wear a pair of splotch pants but I wouldn't. He dresses funny. His socks don't always match and sometimes his pants are too short.

Calvin

We walk quietly for a while. Then, when we get to the big tree near school he says, "I hope those splotches don't mean you're through with the experiment."

I tell him I'm willing to go on.

"But today I'm eating some. I can't sit through class all day, smell those beans and not nibble."

24

Calvin shakes his head and says, "Nibble! Nibble! Nibble. Did Thomas Edison's light bulbs nibble their filaments? And what about Alexander Graham Bell and Chester Greenwood? Did they have to worry about nibbling?"

"Chester Greenwood?"

"He invented earmuffs."

"Oh," I say and nibble on a red bean.

I promise not to eat too many beans and we go to class.

Mrs. Cakel is talking and I'm doodling. Doodling is good practice if you want to be a cartoonist. And then it happens again. The ice cream gets in trouble with the onion.

The lesson was on fractions and Mrs. Cakel asks Calvin, "How much is one half plus one quarter?"

He thinks for a moment and then answers, "Tallahassee is the capital of Florida."

Mrs. Cakel stares at Calvin.

He smiles.

"Remain after class."

She means during lunch, that she wants to talk to him. Calvin won't be able to watch me. That will skew his experiment, so I skew too. I eat another red bean.

At lunch Annie tells me she started working on the Washington report. "I'm doing the president part," she says. "You'll do the soldier stuff."

Annie is bossy.

"Tell Alvin not to fool around with his report," Douglas says. "I'm not getting a bad grade because of him."

"He wouldn't do that," I say.

But I'm not sure.

"And tell him I want some green jelly beans," Annie says.

I have an idea.

"By this weekend his experiment will be done. Maybe we can all go to his house on Sunday and have a jelly bean party."

"I want oranges," Douglas says. "Oranges are loaded with vitamin C."

"Mom always tells me to eat my greens," Annie says. "Greens have lots of vitamins."

I'm sure they're joking.

I wait, but neither of them laughs.

"Oranges that grow on trees have vitamin C," I tell Douglas and Annie. "Green vegetables have vitamins. Orange and green jelly beans just have lots of sugar."

"Well, I still like greens," Annie says. "Tell Calvin if he saves me the greens, I'll come to his house."

Douglas says he would come too, if Calvin saves him orange beans. He also says, "We can also work on our report."

On the way home I ask Calvin why he answered Tallahassee to a question on fractions.

"I didn't hear the question. I didn't even know we were doing math and most teachers like capitals and everyone loves Florida."

That makes sense.

"She made me eat my lunch in the room."

I tell Calvin the good news, that Annie and Douglas will come to his party. I also tell him we have to get started on our reports.

"I'll do an Internet search," Calvin says, "and I'll get books from the library."

He stops walking and asks, "Where's the library?"

"We'll go there together," I say. "My sister Karen can take us."

He looks at me. He's studying me.

"What?" I ask.

"Your sister makes you feel inadequate."

"Inadequate?"

"Like you're not as smart as she is, not as good as she is."

Why did he say that?

"It's your shoulders. When you told me she would take us to the library your shoulders slumped a bit."

I told you he's weird.

That afternoon Karen walks with us to the library.

She asks Calvin lots of questions.

"Why do you wear different color socks?"

"My feet are different. The right one is very serious. It likes solid blue socks. My left foot is often silly and likes colorful stripes."

Karen

Karen stops. We are still a few blocks from the library. She puts her hands on her hips, looks right at Calvin, and tells him, "It's not your left foot that's silly. It's you."

Karen looks him over.

"And why is your hair combed all the way back? Only old men wear their hair like that."

"That's obviously not true," Calvin tells her. "This is how I comb my hair and I'm just ten."

Karen shakes her head and we continue walking.

We stop at the corner and Karen asks, "Is your father really a spy?"

I had told her that.

"I can't talk about it." He looks up and down the street and then whispers, "He's on a secret mission."

Karen shakes her head. She doesn't believe the spy stuff.

At the library I learn some really interesting things about George Washington. Did you know that his wife Martha knitted socks for the American soldiers? She also helped patch their torn clothes.

Calvin tells me that Benjamin Franklin did lots of experiments with electricity. Once he grabbed two wires, one in each hand, and *boom*! He had a terrible shock.

Benjamin Franklin
is shocked.

"That friend of yours is a little strange." Karen tells me when we get home. "But so are you."

Karen is strange too.

Chapter 4

SUNDAY AND IT'S GOOD

Karen is in the eighth grade. That's almost high school.

Last week she was on a yellow diet. She only ate pineapple, lemon meringue pie, yellow squash, corn, chicken, chickpeas, and bananas. This week she's on a string diet. She eats string beans, string cheese, string licorice, and spaghetti.

At dinner Karen refuses

to eat grilled tuna until Dad cuts it into long stringy pieces.

"This is too weird," Mom says. "These diets aren't healthy.

"You are what you eat," Karen says.

She says that a lot.

I put down my fork and tell her, "That's true. Right now you're a yellow string with large brown eyes and curly hair."

"Yes, I am," Karen says likes she's proud of it.

It's Thursday morning and I think about how Karen doesn't believe that Calvin's dad is a spy. On our way to school I ask Calvin, "What's with your dad?"

"Sh!" Calvin says.

He holds his pointing finger in front of his mouth.

"I can't talk about him."

"Do you know where he is?"

"If I told you that I would be talking about him. And I can't."

So I tell him about my dad. He sells plumbing supplies. People don't like to talk about pipes and toilets but like Dad says, "We sure need them."

When we get close to school, I ask Calvin when his experiment will be done.

"Friday."

That's tomorrow.

"Then I'll tally the results."

He loads my pockets with beans and we go to class.

Mrs. Cakel changes Calvin's seat. She puts him right by her desk. I think she wants to be able to watch him closely.

"Read," she tells him during silent reading.

"I am."

"No, you're not."

Sweet Mrs. Cakel

Calvin leans closer to his book. After a minute or so he turns the page.

"That's better," Mrs. Cakel says.

How does she know if he's reading?

"Was she right?" I ask Calvin on our way to lunch.

"Yeah," he says. "I wasn't reading and then I was. But that woman doesn't know everything."

He sticks out his tongue. There's gum on it.

"I was chewing all morning."

Mrs. Cakel hates gum chewing and Calvin knows it. He sure likes to live dangerously.

Spies live dangerously. Maybe when his dad was in fourth grade he pretended to read when he wasn't. Maybe he chewed gum in class. Maybe his teacher was Mrs. Cakel. She's old enough.

℗ ℗ ℗

It's Friday. At lunch Douglas looks to where Calvin is sitting and says, "He's still watching us."

"This is the last day of the experiment."

Douglas shivers.

"It's creepy," he says. "I don't like someone watching me when I eat."

Douglas turns so his back is to Calvin. He doesn't want Calvin to see him. He bends forward. I can't see what Douglas is doing. At first he has a sandwich and then he doesn't so I guess he's eating.

On the way home I tell Calvin what Douglas said.

"He should get used to it," Calvin tells me. "Cameras are everywhere. They're in banks, and post offices, and the lobbies of apartment buildings. I even saw one in a pizza shop and do you know what I did?"

I shake my head. I don't know.

"I looked right at the camera and opened my mouth. Have you ever seen a mouthful of half-chewed mushroom pizza?"

35

I shake my head again. I never saw that and I don't want to.

We're at the corner waiting to cross the street. I ask about the party.

"What food will you have?"

"Cake, juice, soda, and ice cream."

I don't ask about the beans. They've been in and out of my pockets all week. They're sticky, dirty, and some have pocket lint stuck to them.

"Strawberry," Calvin says. "I told Mom to get an interesting flavor of ice cream and she got strawberry."

"I like strawberry," I tell him.

I remind him that our reports are due on Monday.

"Annie, Douglas, and I are bringing our books and notes to the party."

Calvin tells me, "Strawberries are not really berries."

"Don't fool around with the report. That wouldn't be fair to Douglas."

"That's because real berries have their seeds on the inside and strawberries have them on the outside."

"I hope you know something about Benjamin Franklin."

"He liked strawberries. Everyone likes strawberries."

When I get home, I work on my report. I want to get it done. I also think I'm lucky not to have Calvin as my partner.

It's berry nice to meet you

☺ ☺ ☺

It's Sunday. Calvin's party is at two. I go early. His mother opens the door.

"Hello," she says. "You must be here for Calvin."

I stand there and look at her.

37

Mrs. Waffle

She's real skinny and has long, curly red hair. Her shirt and pants are real colorful, lots of stripes and dots.

"Come in. Come in," she says.

She says that a bit too loud.

"I hope you like chocolate cake and ice cream. Sure, you do. Everyone likes cake and ice cream. Most people like vanilla. Did you know that? But we don't have vanilla. We have strawberry. It's pink. I like the color but I don't like the flavor. I hope you do."

She talks real fast.

"Calvin!" she shouts.

I follow her into a large room.

There are a few folding beach chairs in the room and a television on a large box. There is a long narrow table with photographs in picture frames. On the floor are lots of magazines.

She talks some more about ice cream.

"I got strawberry because of Calvin. He said to get an interesting flavor. They had pistachio but that's green. Green ice cream! I once lost a sandwich. It was under my bed. I don't know how it got there but it turned green. Mold. I don't eat green sandwiches and I don't eat green ice cream."

Someone says, "Hey, Danny."

I turn. It's Calvin.

"You're early."

"I came to help you get ready."

He leads me into the kitchen.

Four beach chairs are next to a small table. In the middle of the table is a large chocolate cake, paper plates and cups, and plastic forks.

Calvin says, "There's not much to do for the party. The ice cream is in the freezer. The juice and soda are in the refrigerator."

"Then let's talk about our reports. Mine is in this folder," I say.

I know Douglas and Annie want us to work on our reports today. That's why I brought mine with me.

It's all written out so if I get nervous I can just read it.

I stand. I look at Calvin, smile, and read from my report.

"George Washington, soldier."

Washington is in the middle of the Revolutionary War when the doorbell rings.

Calvin and I open the door. Annie and Douglas are standing there. Annie has an armload of papers and books. Douglas has a bat, a ball, and two gloves.

"What's with the baseball stuff?" I ask.

"Big game Tuesday," Douglas tells me as he walks past us and into the

Annie

house. "I'm pitching and I need to practice. You'll catch."

"I'll catch too," Annie says. "I'm good."

Annie thinks she's good at everything.

"Who says we'll catch?" Calvin asks. "This is my house and my party. I'll decide what we do."

Calvin crisscrosses his arms.

He stares at Douglas.

Douglas stares back.

Calvin uncrosses his arms, points at Douglas, and says, "First we'll work on our reports. Then we'll party. Maybe then we'll catch stuff. And that's final!"

"Yeah, let's go," Douglas says. "I gotta show you all my new pitch. It's a killer."

Annie is still by the doorway. "I hope you did your report," she says to me.

"It's seven pages," I tell her.

"Mine is twelve pages, and it's good."

Chapter 5

STILL SUNDAY AND THE BATHROOM SPY

"I'll go first," Annie says.

She holds a folder with one hand. She drops the books she has in her other hand on one of the beach chairs. The chair folds and collapses.

"Good start," Douglas says.

"George Washington was the first president of the United States. He was inaugurated in New York City on April 30, 1789."

That's how she starts.

Boring!

She tells us the population of the United States and how many of them were men, women, children, and slaves. She tells us how many people lived in each state. She goes on and on with names and dates and numbers. While Annie talks, I look at the magazines on the floor. They're mostly gossip magazines. On the cover of each one is a picture of some famous person. *Pictures!*

I look at the photographs on the table. There are pictures of Calvin and his mother. I look again. There are *only* pictures of Calvin and his mother. There is no picture of a man, someone who might be Calvin's father.

PUZZLE
GUYS

"Samuel Osgood was Washington's first Postmaster General," Annie says. "He was born in Andover, Massachusetts."

Maybe Calvin's father really is a spy and it wouldn't be safe to have his picture where

44

anyone could see it. Maybe his father died or ran off. Maybe Calvin never met him.

I don't like to be nosy. Calvin's father is really none of my business.

Annie says, "Timothy Pickering was the second Postmaster General. He was from Salem, Massachusetts."

But I'm curious.

"Joseph Habersham was Washington's third Postmaster General. He was from Savannah, Georgia."

A bathroom is a good place to find out about someone. I decide to check out the Waffle family bathroom.

"That's it," Annie says. She closes her folder. "Who's next?"

Not me, I think. My report is nothing like Annie's, and since we're partners she'll tell me it's no good, that I have to do it over. She'll want me to put in all kinds of names and numbers.

Douglas stands.

"My report is about Benjamin Franklin, about his years as a statesman."

He opens his folder. He looks at his papers and then looks up.

"I've got lots of interesting stuff here, but I don't want to read it. I want to eat."

"Yeah," I say. "Let's eat."

We follow Calvin into the kitchen. His mom is there.

A pot of jelly beans

"Who wants ice cream?" she asks. "It's pink."

"It's strawberry," Calvin explains.

We have juice, milk, and ice cream. Annie asks about the jelly beans.

Calvin opens a cabinet and takes out a large pot. It's filled with beans.

"Me first," Annie says. "I want the green ones."

She reaches in the pot and picks out several green beans.

"Yuck! These are dirty. There's thread and lint on them."

The ones with thread must have been in my shirt pocket.

"Put them back and I'll wash them," Calvin says.

Annie puts her green beans back, and Calvin puts the pot in the sink. He fills the pot with water.

"Did you tally the results? Do you have the statistics?" I ask. "Why did you fill my pockets with beans?"

"It was a social experiment," Calvin says as he drains the water out of the pot. He puts it in the middle of the kitchen table.

"Smell the beans."

Douglas takes a deep breath.

"Ah!"

Annie stands. She leans forward. She sticks her nose in the pot. She has long blond hair. It falls in the pot.

Annie takes a deep breath.

"Ah! I love that sweet smell."

"That's it! The sweet smell," Calvin tells us.

"I wanted to see if people would be attracted to Danny if he smelled like jelly beans."

"Who wants brown and yellow cake?" Calvin's mother asks.

"It's chocolate with buttercream," Calvin explains.

"It's good," Calvin's mother says. "When it was in the oven, I licked the batter bowl and that was *real* good. If you have a good batter, you'll have a good cake. I was a good batter. When I was younger I played little league and I could really hit. I had two home runs in one game."

I bet if Mrs. Waffle was our age, she would join the Eagles. Maybe she can bring Calvin to a game.

A bowl of batter

Mrs. Waffle gives each of us a piece of cake. She's right. It is good.

Calvin tells us about his experiment.

"I watched him for one week when he smelled like Danny."

Smelled like Danny! What does that mean?

"Then I watched him with the beans. And do you know what? Kids liked the bean smell. Twelve percent more people spoke to him during the jelly bean week. And they talked to him longer."

"They did?"

"I'm going to make jelly bean perfume— JBP. That's what I'll call it. You spray it on in the morning and you'll be popular all day."

"Could you make it in different flavors?" Annie asks. "I want green bean perfume."

"This is all too weird," Douglas says. "Whoever heard of people smelling like jelly beans?"

"Weird? Is that what people said to Alexander Graham Bell when he invented the telephone? Is that what they said to Thomas Edison when he invented the light bulb?"

Jelly Bean Perfume

49

"Those things changed people's lives," I say.

"JBP will change people's lives. Kids who keep moving to different schools will spray on JBP and have lots of friends."

Now Calvin is talking about himself.

Douglas holds his half-eaten slice of chocolate cake to his nose. He takes a deep breath.

"This smells so good," he says. "How about making chocolate cake perfume?"

"You could call it CCP, Chocolate Cake Perfume," Annie says. "You could advertise it in magazines and on the Web. I'll be the model."

Annie walks slowly around the kitchen like she's a fashion model. And then I see them.

"Annie," I say. "You've got jelly beans in your hair."

"What?"

A red bean and a yellow are stuck to her. That must have happened when she put her nose in the pot.

She grabs the ends of her hair and looks at the beans.

"Yuck! I've got to go to the bathroom and wash these out."

"The bathroom," I say. "I've got to go there too."

"Come with me," Mrs. Waffle tells us. "I'll show you where it is."

We walk with her through the large room by the front door.

"I'm changing the bathroom wallpaper," she says. "It's not hard. You just have to brush on the paste, smooth out the paper, and match the seams. But things are not always what they seem. This town seems like a good place to live. What do you think?"

"It's nice here," Annie tells her.

"Here's the bathroom," Mrs. Waffle says. "But there's no bath. It's really a shower room."

"You go first," Annie tells me. "I can wait and maybe you can't."

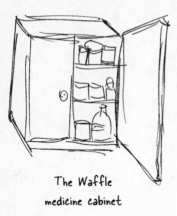

The Waffle
medicine cabinet

I go in and close the door. Taped to the wall above the sink are a few squares of wallpaper. I guess Mrs. Waffle hasn't decided which one she likes.

I open the medicine cabinet and look for some evidence that a man lives in the house. There are tubes of weird colors of lipstick, face powder, a jar of roll-on deodorant, and lilac room spray. There is no shaver and no shaving cream.

There are a few pill jars.

I look at the labels. Three are for Alice Waffle. One is for Calvin.

There are just two towels by the shower, a red and a blue.

I open the shower door. I see the same stuff Mom has in her shower, shampoo and conditioner that smells like flowers, but none of the stuff Dad has.

"What are you doing in there?" Annie asks.

"I'm done," I say.

I flush the toilet, turn on the cold water faucet, wash my hands, and dry them. Then I open the door.

"It's all yours," I say.

Annie leans into the bathroom. She takes a deep breath.

"Good," she says. "You didn't smell it up."

She goes in and closes the door.

I think about the no shaver and no shaving cream. I'm not sure what that proves. Maybe that means there is no Mr. Waffle. Or maybe it means Mr. Waffle is a clever spy and took out any evidence that he lives in this house.

I go back to the kitchen. Calvin and Douglas are talking. Calvin has made a friend without spraying on any JBP.

Mrs. Waffle is standing by the sink. She's eating cake.

53

We never eat the jelly beans. After Calvin washed them, they became just a sticky multicolored lump. We just talk.

Calvin stands by the kitchen table and says, "Guess who I am."

He looks right at Annie and tells her, "Sit straight."

Annie sits up.

"Straight," Calvin says and holds up a pencil. "This is straight. Sit like this. Sit like a pencil."

Calvin pretending to be a pencil

"I can't do that."

"You can't or you won't? The pencil can do it. My ruler can do it. The door can do it."

Annie, Douglas, and I laugh. Mrs. Waffle doesn't.

"How can someone sit like a pencil?" she asks.

"Look at that sign," Calvin says and points to the refrigerator. "Sit straight like a pencil. Be quiet like a book. No talking. No mumbling. No chewing. No breathing."

"What sign?" Mrs. Waffle asks.

"He's pretending to be Mrs. Cakel," I tell her. "She's our teacher and she has a big NO sign in our classroom."

"Just watch," Calvin says. "I'll be chewing gum tomorrow when I give my report."

"No," Douglas says. "It's not *your* report. It's *our* report. I worked hard on it. I want a good grade."

"We'll get a good grade, and she'll never know I'm chewing." Calvin smiles and adds, "I have my ways."

Chapter 6

MORE SUNDAY AND CALVIN READS PEOPLE

"We did our report stuff," Douglas says. "We had the party. Now let's go outside, and I'll show you my new pitch."

"We'll all go," Mrs. Waffle says. "And give Calvin the bat. He'll hit."

"No, Ma."

"Yes. When you were younger, you were real good at hitting. You hit baseballs. You hit great shots at miniature golf. You even hit the bull's-eye with your toy bow and arrow." Then she explains to us, "The bull's-eye is the small circle in the middle of the target. Hey," she says to Calvin, "There's a sale at Target. Do you need new shirts or pants or underclothes?"

"Ma!"

"Your friends know about underclothes. Don't you?"

She looks right at me when she asks that, but I don't answer.

Douglas gives me a glove and tells me to catch. "You'll hit first," he tells Calvin and gives him the bat, "only you won't be able to hit my pitches. Annie, you'll go next."

He drops his notebook on the front lawn and says, "This will be home plate."

Douglas counts aloud as he takes twenty big steps across the front walk to the other side of the lawn. He drops a twig at his feet and says, "I'll throw from here. This is the pitcher's mound."

I crouch behind the notebook.

Douglas

58

Calvin holds the bat back and waits.

It actually looks like Calvin has played baseball before.

Mrs. Waffle stands behind me "I'm the umpire," she says, "even though umpires are mostly fat, dress in black, and wear sensible shoes."

Mrs. Waffle is wearing sensible sandals and not so sensible rainbow-striped socks.

Annie stands a few steps behind Douglas. She's the fielder.

Douglas leans back. He swings his arms around and throws the ball. It comes toward me real fast. That's why he's our team's pitcher. He can throw real fast. The ball is high, way too high to be a good pitch. I have to jump to catch it.

"Ball one," Mrs. Waffle calls.

I throw the ball back to Douglas.

He does it again. He leans back. He swings his arms around and throws the ball.

I expect another fast ball, but this pitch is much slower than the first one and closer to the plate. But not close enough.

"Ball two," Mrs. Waffle calls.

"Did you see that? Did you see it?" Douglas asks as he hurries toward me. "That's my new pitch. It's a change-up. It looks like I'm throwing a fastball, but I'm not. It will sure fool the batter. He'll swing early and miss."

Douglas goes back to the twig.

"It won't fool me," Calvin says quietly.

Douglas leans back. He swings his arms around and throws the ball.

"Fastball," Calvin whispers.

He's right. The ball comes in real fast. Calvin swings and misses.

"Strike one," Mrs. Waffle calls.

I throw the ball back to Douglas. He catches it. Then he leans back, swings his arms around, and throws it again.

"Slow ball," Calvin whispers.

He's right.

Calvin waits. Then, just as the ball is about to cross the plate, he swings and hits the ball way over Douglas's head.

Douglas and Annie chase after it.

"Nice hit," I tell Calvin. "How did you know it would be a change-up?"

"He told me."

"Who told you?"

"Douglas did. Before he throws a fastball, he holds his glove against his stomach. Before a slow pitch, he doesn't."

Mrs. Waffle says, "Calvin reads people. I don't. I read fan magazines. Did you know that every morning Angie Bell eats a fish sandwich? She says it gives her energy."

I eat oatmeal

I eat a fish sandwich

Douglas has the ball. He's standing on the twig.

Mrs. Waffle says, "Paulie Peterson eats oatmeal. They had a great story on what stars eat for breakfast."

"My turn to bat," Annie says.

I watch as Douglas leans back. He holds the glove against his stomach, swings his arms around, and throws the ball real fast. Annie swings the bat and misses.

He does it again. He holds the glove against his stomach, swings his arms around and throws the ball.

"Fastball," I tell Annie.

Annie swings and hits the ball over Douglas's head.

Douglas pitches again and again, and each time we know exactly what he's going to throw. And Mrs. Waffle tells me what all the stars eat. Someone has chocolate and buttermilk every morning. I forget who.

Douglas throws down his glove. He's angry. "How do you keep hitting me?"

Calvin tells him about his glove and his stomach and how he signals his pitches.

"Calvin reads people," Mrs. Waffle tells him. "I read fan magazines."

And I say, "If Calvin knows what you're about to throw, the other team will also know."

Douglas practices throwing his new pitch, but now, before he throws, he rests his glove against his stomach.

He throws lots of pitches, some fast and some what he calls his "new super-duper change-up." Now even Calvin can't tell what he's about to pitch.

Mrs. Waffle comes out carrying a tray. On it are four paper bowls of brown and yellow cake, each with a scoop of pink ice cream on top.

We talk while we eat, and Annie has an idea.

"If Calvin could read Douglas's pitches, why can't he read the pitches of the other team?"

Douglas says, "The Robins have a great pitcher. He throws a fastball, a change-up, and a curve."

Mrs. Waffle asks, "Would it help if you knew which pitch was coming?"

"Sure, it would help."

"But is that right?" I ask. "We'd be taking advantage of the other team's pitcher."

"Of course it's right," Douglas says. "If the other pitcher tells us what he's going to throw, why shouldn't we listen?"

"I don't know," I say.

Slider... bla ... bla ... bla ... bla...

"Haven't you ever watched a game on TV?" Douglas asks. "When the pitcher talks to the catcher, he holds his glove in front of his face. That's so the other team can't read his lips and know what he's saying. Teams try to read lips, so we can try to read body language."

"Can you do it?" Annie asks Calvin.

"Sure. It will be like an experiment."

Mrs. Waffle brings out what's left of the cake. She tells us to finish it. I take a small piece.

"There's something else," Calvin says. He turns to Annie and tells her, "You really like Danny."

Annie blushes, and so do I.

Why does he do that? I was beginning to think Calvin is a great guy with an unusual talent, and then he embarrasses me.

Calvin tells Annie, "When you look at him, the corners of your lips move up a bit, like you're about to smile."

Calvin says Annie likes me

This party lasted about five minutes too long.

I should have said, "No, thank you," when Mrs. Waffle offered me more cake. I should have said, "I need to go home."

I should have left.

But I didn't.

Now Annie's face is as pink as the strawberry ice cream, and I think so is mine.

Chapter 7

SUNDAY, MONDAY, AND WHAT ABOUT MR. WAFFLE?

"This morning when I was shopping," Mom says at dinner, "I met your friend's mother. She was buying juice and soda and paper plates for the party."

I have a mouth full of mashed potatoes, so I don't answer. I just nod.

Karen is cutting her chicken cutlet into long thin pieces. She is still on her string diet.

"Did she tell you there was a spy in the family?" Karen asks.

"She told me lots of things. She can really talk. First she told me she bought orange juice for the party so she couldn't buy cherry soda. That's because the colors orange and red clash. 'I have what people call red hair,' she said, 'but it's really more orange than red, so I don't wear red shirts.' Then she told me ginger ale was OK because that's yellow."

Karen asks, "What about Mr. Waffle?"

"She said it's been real hard for them after he ran off."

"Is he a spy?"

"He works for a trucking company. He's a driver."

Karen says, "I knew he wasn't a spy."

I don't say anything, but I knew it too.

I think about that all night, that Calvin had lied to me. But the next morning I don't say anything about it. I talk about our reports.

"Don't do it," I tell Calvin on our way to school. "You'll get in big trouble if you chew gum."

"Smell me," Calvin says.

"What?"

"Smell me."

I smell his shirt.

"I'm wearing JBP. I made a whole lot of it. I put it in an empty lemon spray-cleaner jar, and this morning I sprayed it on."

He holds his arm in front of me. It smells sweet. Then I touch his arm. It's sticky.

"I sprayed it on after my shower. I'm covered with sweet-smelling JBP."

I push his shirt against his chest, and it sticks to him. He pulls it off his chest, and we go into school.

Mrs. Cakel checks our homework.

She teaches us some math.

We give our reports.

Janet and Carol are first. Their report is on Louis Braille. He invented the raised dot alphabet that blind people use for reading. He did that when he was fifteen. Janet and Carol show us a braille book, and I get to feel the braille dots.

Perry and Michael report on Helen Keller.

Annie and I go next. I go first because my report is on Washington's early years.

Mrs. Cakel stands in the back of the room. Calvin is right in front, right by her desk. I'm standing there, and Calvin opens his mouth, sticks out his tongue, and shows me a huge wad of gum.

I bite my tongue to stop from laughing.

Throughout my report Calvin smiles at me and opens his mouth.

George Washington was tall. Here he is playing basketball.

I try not to look at him, but it's difficult. He's right there in front.

I'm done, and it's Annie's turn. She talks on and on about Washington as president.

"That was an excellent report," Mrs. Cakel tells Annie and me when we're done. "We'll continue after lunch."

The bell rings.

"Calvin," Mrs. Cakel says as we're leaving the room. "Wait here. I want to talk to you."

She got him!

All through class he had his back to her. She was all the way in the back of the room. I don't know how she saw what he was doing, but *she has her ways*!

For lunch I sit at my usual table.

Douglas tells me, "You looked like you were in real pain up there."

I tell him and Annie what Calvin was doing.

Douglas throws up his hands. "How did I get stuck with him? I'm going to fail my report. He's always in trouble."

"It's your parents' fault," I say.

"What?"

"You got Calvin because your last name is Miller. You were

the last to pick. All the kids ahead of you in the alphabet already had partners."

"He's right," Annie says. "My name is Abrams. I always go first."

Calvin walks into the cafeteria. He comes to our table.

"She caught you," I say. "I tell you, that woman knows everything."

"No, she doesn't," Calvin says.

He sticks out his tongue. There's gum on it.

"What did she want?" I ask. "Why did she tell you to stay after class?"

"She wanted to know how I was doing. She wanted to know if I enjoyed working with you, Douglas. She also said we're giving our report right after lunch."

I say, "She was being nice. Wow!"

"It's the JBP. I'm wearing it, and it's working. It even attracted grumpy Mrs. Cakel."

Calvin takes the gum out of his mouth. He puts it on his forehead. Then he opens his lunch bag and takes out his sandwich. He peels back the top piece of bread.

"Banana and marshmallow," he says. "I made it myself, and it's delicious."

"Don't forget tomorrow's game," Annie tells him. "We need to win, and we're counting on you to help."

Calvin nods and gives us a big, gooey, banana-marshmallow smile.

The lunch period ends, and Calvin takes the gum off his forehead. He puts it back in his mouth, and we go to class.

Mrs. Cakel is in front of the room.

"This morning's reports were excellent. This afternoon we begin with Calvin Waffle, Douglas Miller, and Benjamin Franklin."

Calvin takes the report folder

IT'S SHOE TIME!

off his desk. Mrs. Cakel walks toward the back of the room and while she has her back to us, Calvin opens his mouth wide. He sticks out his tongue and shows us a big wad of gum. A few kids laugh. Douglas shakes his head and puts it down on his desk. He isn't happy.

"Benjamin Franklin was born in 1706 in Boston in a house on Milk Street. Maybe it was called Milk Street because lots of people kept cows in their yards."

That's a good beginning.

Douglas looks up.

"They also kept pigs and chickens in their yards, so I guess people had to be careful when they walked outside."

Ben Franklin's neighbors

Calvin lifts his right foot. He looks at the bottom of his shoe and pretends he stepped in cow pie. He wrinkles his nose, wipes his shoe, and goes on with his report.

Douglas shakes his head and puts it down on his desk again.

Calvin talks a lot about Franklin's experiments. I already knew that with a kite and a key he proved that lightning was electricity. I didn't know he used electricity to kill chickens and turkeys for his dinner.

"Excellent," Mrs. Cakel says when he's done.

Douglas's report is good, too.

Calvin is in a great mood on the way home. He talks and talks. I guess in that way he's like his mother.

"Franklin kept experimenting with electricity. Edison kept experimenting with light bulbs. And I'll keep experimenting with jelly beans. One day, kids will be writing reports on the experiments of Calvin Waffle."

I don't think so.

"There will be jelly bean–powered cars."

"Jelly beans are sugar," I tell him, "and sugar will ruin a car engine."

We're at the corner nearest his house. Calvin stops. He points up and says, "Aha!"

"Aha what?"

"Cars use ethanol. That's made with corn. Corn is a starch. Sugar is a starch. That's the 'aha.'"

"I'm just saying, don't put jelly beans in any car engine. You'll ruin it."

"I'll just have to invent a new type of engine."

I'm about to tell Calvin he's loopy when I remember Washington Carver. Maybe Carver spoke about his plans for peanuts and someone told him *he* was loopy. That someone would have been wrong.

We start walking again.

"What happened with your gum?"

"Today was the first time she said anything

nice to me. She hardly ever says anything nice to anyone. I didn't want to ruin that. Just before I started the report, I swallowed the gum. With all the gum and marshmallow, my whole insides are probably stuck together."

I think he's joking, but I'm not sure. And I'm still not sure Annie and Douglas were joking about orange and green jelly beans being good for you.

"The gum didn't go down easy," Calvin says, "but Dad told me a spy must know when to abandon a mission."

His dad!

"I didn't want to get in trouble and I didn't want Douglas to get a bad grade because of me."

"Yeah," I say. "He's your friend. Annie is too."

"You're my best friend," Calvin says. "So I can tell you this."

Calvin looks around. He leans close. He is about to tell me a secret.

YOU DON'T SEE ME.

I AM CALVIN'S FATHER. I AM A...spy...

"Every spy has a cover," he whispers. "Something he tells the real world that isn't really true. You know, he can't tell his doctor or his butcher that he's a spy."

"So what does your dad say?"

"He tells people he's a truck driver. That's his cover."

"Oh," I say.

What else could I say?

If it's his cover, that's what Mrs. Waffle would tell people he does. Of course, if he's really a truck driver who ran off, that's also what she would say.

We walk until we're in front of his house.

"Don't forget tomorrow's game," I tell him. "It's an important game. My mom is taking me. You can come with us."

"OK," Calvin says. "Unless I get a call from my dad. He calls whenever he gets a safe phone, you know, one that's not bugged."

"Yeah," I say. "I know."

Only I don't know.

I walk down the block to my house and think about Calvin. Maybe his dad *is* a spy. And maybe he's not. Either way, it's OK with me. Friends don't ask questions. We just fill our pockets with jelly beans, help with experiments, walk together, eat lunch together, and listen.

Chapter 8

~~~~~~~~~~~~~~~~~~~~~~~~~~~~~~~~

TUESDAY AND THE BIG GAME

The field we play on is just a few blocks away, so we don't drive there. We walk. It's me, Mom, Dad, Calvin, and Mrs. Waffle. Mrs. Waffle talks the whole way.

"I need a job and I like to bake, so I'm thinking of getting a job in a bakery."

"That's nice," Mom says, but that doesn't stop Mrs. Waffle.

"I could make cheese buns or cream puffs, but I wouldn't puff cigarettes. That's bad for you. Do you know what else is bad for you? Burnt meat. And it's so hard to meet people and make friends when you move. I'm really glad we met."

We get to the field. Some of the Robins are already practicing.

"I once met someone named Napoleon Smith," Mrs. Waffle says. "Isn't that an odd name? Not Smith. That's not odd. Napoleon. I think that's an odd name to give a child. And do you know there's a pastry called Napoleon? It's flaky and sweet with lots of cream."

"Number Fourteen," I tell Calvin. "He's the Robins' pitcher."

We spot him. He's near the stands and he's throwing to Robins' Number Eight. I think Eight is their catcher. Calvin and I sit a few rows up and watch. Calvin's mother sits in the first row with my parents.

The Robins' pitcher is tall and skinny, with real long arms and legs. And he looks like he's in high school. Under

his nose he has what looks like the
beginning of a mustache.

At first, Fourteen throws softly to
Eight. Then he throws harder.

"He's warming up," I whisper.

We watch for a while. Number
Eight crouches. He holds his glove
up, just like a catcher. He drops the
hand without the glove between his
legs, wiggles his fingers, and waits.

Fourteen has his glove on one hand.
He holds the ball with his other hand. First
he holds his hands against his stomach. He
reaches over his head, swings both arms
around, and throws the ball to Eight.

Yikes!

He's so skinny, and his uniform must be about
three sizes too big for him. When he swings his
arms around, the sleeves of his uniform flap
like there's a hurricane coming. Then, out of
that flapping white uniform comes the small

83

white ball. It must be almost impossible to hit against him.

Mom turns and looks up at me. "Why don't you throw a ball around?" she asks.

"Yeah," Dad says. "You need to get loose before the game."

Mrs. Waffle looks at my mother. She looks at my father and says, "Hey, I just thought of something. The word 'loose' has two Os. If you take out one O, you have 'lose.' That means, if you're not completely loose you lose."

Huh?

"Dad's right," Mom says. "You should do something to get ready for the game."

"I will," I tell her. "But right now we're busy."

Mom looks at me. She doesn't think Calvin and I can be busy if all we're doing is sitting in the stands. But we *are* busy. We're watching the Robins' Number Fourteen.

Mom, Dad, and Mrs. Waffle turn and face

the field. They talk. Actually, Mrs. Waffle talks. My parents just sit there. I wonder if she's still talking about flaky pastries.

We continue to watch the Robins' pitcher warm up.

"He has three pitches," I whisper to Calvin, "a fastball, a change-up, and a curve."

After each pitch I tell Calvin what Fourteen threw.

"Fastball."

"Fastball."

"Change-up."

"Curve."

"Fastball."

"Change-up."

"I think I have it," Calvin whispers.

I watch as Fourteen holds his hands against his stomach. He reaches over his head, swings both hands around, and throws the ball.

"Curve," Calvin whispers just as the ball leaves Fourteen's hand.

He's right!

Number Fourteen does it again. He holds his hands against his stomach, reaches over his head, swings both hands around, and throws the ball.

"Change-up," Calvin whispers.

He's right again!

"Watch his eyebrows," Calvin tells me. "They just sit there on his face when it's going to be a fastball. They arch up before a change-up. They squinch together before a curve."

"Let's go! Let's go!" my coach calls. He's looking straight at me. "Don't just sit there. Throw a ball around. Limber up."

"Let's go," I tell Calvin.

He shakes his head and says, "You go. I'm not on the team."

I join Douglas and Annie and we limber.

Okay, so I'm not exactly sure what "limber"

means. What I do is stretch my arms and legs. I swing my arms all around, like a sideways helicopter. I arch my back. I think that's limbering.

"Watch me," Douglas says.

I watch him and Annie warm up for the game. Each time, before Douglas throws the ball, he holds his glove against his stomach, even before his new super-duper change-up. I can't tell what kind of pitch he's about to throw.

Thank you, Calvin Waffle.

The game starts.

By the second inning, when it's finally my turn to bat, we're already losing. 2–0. There are two outs, and Annie is on second base.

I stand by home plate, hold my bat back, and wait.

There *is* the beginning of a mustache under Fourteen's nose. He must be thirty years old!

Fourteen leans forward. He's checking Number Eight's wiggly fingers to know what to pitch. I watch Fourteen's eyebrows. Nothing.

They're just sitting there on top of his eyes.

Please, Please, don't hit me. Please, don't hurt me!

Fastball.

Fourteen holds his hands against his stomach. He reaches over his head, swings both arms around, and throws the ball.

All I see are flapping shirt sleeves and then a ball speeding toward me. I want to duck. But I don't. The ball comes at me so fast, and I swing late. I have no chance of hitting the ball.

This is no fun.

I watch Fourteen's eyebrows again. Nothing. They just sit there. It's going to be another fastball.

This time I close my eyes and swing.

I miss.

I walk away from the plate. I take a deep breath and walk back.

Number Fourteen has the ball again. He leans in to look at the wiggly fingers. Then his eyebrows move. They arch up. He's going to throw a change-up. That means the ball will come in nice and slow. This time I'll have a chance.

Fourteen holds his hands against his stomach. He reaches over his head, swings both arms around and throws the ball. It looks like it will be a fastball, but it isn't. It comes in nice and slow.

Here goes!

I swing and hit the ball.

Bam!

Okay, so the sound the bat makes when it hits the ball is more like *bing*. But I do hit the ball. It's a bloop just over the third baseman's head. I drop the bat and run.

I run and run. At last, I'm at first base. The third baseman never threw the ball. It was a hit all the way. A mighty bloop! Annie scores.

Thank you, Calvin Waffle.

The next inning, before it's Douglas's turn to bat, I tell him what Calvin discovered. I tell him about the eyebrows. He tells Annie and a few others on the team.

It's so much easier for my team to hit the ball when we know what pitch is coming. We get some hits and score some runs.

By the sixth inning we're behind, 12–11. We only play six innings. This is our last chance.

Number Fourteen is getting a bit wild. Some of his fastballs fly way over the catcher's head. Some bounce before the plate.

This inning he gets two strikeouts.

We get three walks.

It's my turn at bat.

Did you do the math? Two strikeouts and three walks—there are two outs, and the bases are loaded. We're behind by one run.

I stand by the plate, hold my bat back, and wait.

Please, I think. *I don't want to strike out. I don't.*

I watch Fourteen's eyebrows. Nothing. The first pitch will be a fastball. I decide not to swing at it.

Strike one.

Again, I watch the eyebrows. Squinch. Curve. I swing and miss.

This time Fourteen's eyebrows arch up. This will be my pitch, a change-up. Nice and slow.

Fourteen reaches over his head, swings both arms around and throws the ball. His uniform flaps. Now here comes the ball.

I wait for it.

I close my eyes and swing.

Bing!

I open my eyes. This time the ball bloops over the first baseman's head. I run and run. The first baseman runs too. He gets the ball. Now it's just a question of who gets to first base first.

If it's him, I'm out. We lose.

If it's me, it's a hit. At least two runs will score, and we win.

I run till my legs ache. I run till my batting helmet flies off. I run till I reach first base. Yes! I get there just before the first baseman does.

"Safe!" the umpire shouts.

My whole team is running toward me. They're waving their arms and cheering. At least, I think they're cheering. With all the arms waving and all the noise, they could be attacking me.

It's scary!

It's wild!

Yes, wild.

I turn and run the other way. I run past second base and into the outfield. But

Yeah Danny!

yeah!

Yippy! We win!

Yeah!

Yeah Danny!

Hoorah!

yeah! Yippy!

We win! yeah!

Hoorah!

they keep after me. I run back toward the infield and trip over second base. Douglas helps me up.

"You're a hero," Douglas tells me. "You won the game for us."

Douglas and the others on my team pat my back and shake my hand. They want to put me on their shoulders.

"I'm not the hero," I tell them. "He is," I say and point to Calvin. "He reads people and he read their pitcher. I knew what pitch was coming."

CALVIN THE MOVIE STAR

He's standing near the edge of the field. His mother and my parents are with him.

My team turns and looks at Calvin Waffle. We shout and run toward him. Calvin is scared. He runs behind the stands. His mother runs with him.

Mrs. Waffle stops and turns to face us.

"Stop!" she shouts and jumps and waves her arms. "Stop!"

Her curly red hair is flying. Her shirt and pants, all those stripes and dots, are moving, making them a huge colorful blur. And I think of Napoleon, a sweet flaky pastry.

We don't stop.

We run right past Mrs. Waffle. And someone must have bumped her as we run past because she falls to the ground. Douglas and Annie help her up.

At last we catch Calvin. Two of our bigger players hoist him on their shoulders.

"You're a hero," I scream above all the noise.

"I am?" Calvin asks.

I nod my head way up and down like Calvin does when he means yes.

Calvin smiles.

Jelly beans, chewing gum, a silly foot, pink ice cream, and now a hero.

I won't call him weird now.

He's odd.

He's different.

Sometimes different is good.

And now a sneak peek at Danny's next adventure!

DANNY'S DOODLES:
THE DONUT DILEMMA

I'm warning you. I'm about to say two mean and nasty words.

If I say them at school, kids shudder and run away. If I say them at home, my sister Karen says I should be punished for talking dirty.

Are you ready?

Here are the words:

Mrs. Cakel.

She's my teacher and she's super mean and nasty. She makes lunch checks. She won't let us have soda, hard candies, white bread, salty potato chips, cherries, and pomegranate juice.

"I want to keep you healthy," she said, "and I want to keep your clothes from getting horrible red stains."

She won't let Annie Abrams wear her favorite yellow headband.

"It's not becoming," she told Annie.

There are so many rules in our class that my friend Calvin Waffle tells me, "It's lucky she lets us breathe." But, he doesn't tell that to Mrs. Cakel. You can't tell her anything.

Everyone is afraid of Mrs. Cakel.

At open school night, you know, when the teachers tell parents what's wrong with their kids, she told my mother not to slouch, to sit up straight. She told her not to mumble. And do you know what? Mom sat up and spoke up.

Dad was there too.

"I didn't talk to your teacher. I didn't ask her anything," Dad told me later. "I was afraid to."

Once our principal Mr. Telfer walked into our class and he was chewing gum. It was a medicated gum to help him stop smoking. Mrs. Cakel held a garbage can under his chin and made him spit it out. She did that in front of all of us.

And he's the principal!

It's Monday morning. We had lots of homework this weekend and now Mrs. Cakel is checking it. I take mine out of my book bag.

Jason's Lawn Care? Spring clean-up???

This is not my homework. It's the bill from the gardener.

I think about this morning. I had Sugar Flakes for breakfast and they tasted like toothpaste. I hadn't rinsed enough, so I went back to the bathroom, only Karen was in there. I think she does her homework in the bathroom, or something that takes a long time.

I waited.

I finally rinsed and rushed to eat the flakes that no longer tasted like toothpaste, but they were super soggy. I grabbed what I thought was my homework and my lunch and hurried to go to school.

My lunch!

I reach in my desk, take out my lunch bag, and look inside. Lipstick? Mineral body lotion? Face powder? Eyeliner? What is this stuff? Where's my sandwich, pretzels, and apple? I bet right now Mom is sending my homework to the gardener and putting my sandwich in the medicine cabinet.

Here comes Mrs. Cakel.

She'll get bug-eyed when I tell her I don't have my homework. She'll make me copy all the "H" and "W" words in the dictionary. She'll make me stay in class during lunch and do my homework, and the worst part is, she'll be in the room with me. How could I eat while looking at her? I'll lose my appetite.

Oh! I don't have a lunch. All I have is lotion and powder.

She stands by my desk.

"I did my homework," I say, "but I left it at home."

"Bring it in tomorrow," she says and walks to Greg. He sits behind me.

Huh!

Who said that?

It gets worse, or better. I'm not sure if it's good or bad when Mrs. Cakel is nice. I'm not sure it's Mrs. Cakel.

She is teaching us about the American Revolution, you know, when George Washington and the Continental Army fought the British.

She asks my friend Calvin Waffle, "Who fired the first shots at Lexington and Concord?"

"Not me," Calvin answers. "I don't even have a gun."

That's it, I think. *She's really going to explode.*

I hold my hands over my ears. But she doesn't yell. She just calls on Douglas.

"The British fired the first shots," Douglas

answers. "They had lots of guns and fancy red uniforms."

I must be in some alternate universe. Up is down. Big is small. Vinegar is sweet and so is Mrs. Cakel.

I'm a righty, so I try doodling with my left hand. It comes out as just scribble. It's not me! I'm not the one in an alternate universe. Mrs. Cakel is.

The bell rings. It's time for lunch. I buy a container of milk. Then I tell Calvin, Annie, and Douglas about my lunch bagful of lotions and powder and they each give me something to eat.

Annie gives me celery sticks. Douglas gives me some of his pressed fruit roll. And Calvin gives me half of his marshmallow-spread banana sandwich on whole wheat bread. "It tastes better on soft white bread," Calvin says, "but that's against the rules."

My mouth is a sticky mess of marshmallow and fruit roll.

"Shmothang shis wrling," I say.

I wash down some of my weird lunch with milk and try again.

"Something is wrong," I say. "Something is bothering Mrs. Cakel."

"I like her this way," Douglas says, "all sweet and lovey. She's like a kindergarten teacher."

I shake my head.

"No," I say. "We've got to find out what's bothering her. We've got to get back our mean and nasty Mrs. Cakel."

ABOUT THE AUTHOR

David A. Adler, a former math teacher and editor, is the author of more than two hundred books for young readers including the Cam Jansen Mysteries, the entire Picture Book Biography series, and *Don't Talk To Me About the War*. He lives in New York.